Me First

By Ellen Rudin
Illustrated by Richard Walz

For Lauren
—R.N.W.

A GOLDEN BOOK · NEW YORK

Western Publishing Company, Inc., Racine, Wisconsin 53404

Betsy and Bonnie were sisters. They shared the same room. At night they liked to talk to each other as they lay in their beds.

One night Betsy said, "Let's play Me First. We must think of something to do. The one who can do it first is the winner."

"Okay," said Bonnie. She thought for a minute.
Then she said, "Touch the floor!"

Betsy touched the floor first and fell out of bed doing it. "I win!" Betsy said. The sisters giggled.

"Stop that noise," called their mother. "You are supposed to be sleeping."

Bonnie stopped giggling, but Betsy whispered, "We can still play. Whoever wakes up first tomorrow is the winner."

Betsy was sure that she would wake up first, but
when she opened her eyes, Bonnie was staring at her.
"Ha, ha," laughed Bonnie. "I win!"

Betsy got out of bed. She felt jealous of Bonnie
because she wanted to be the winner. "Let's keep
playing," said Betsy. "Brush teeth!" she shouted.
Then she pushed past Bonnie and ran to the
bathroom.

"Hey!" said Bonnie. "You don't have to push!"

Betsy brushed her teeth so fast, the water and
toothpaste went everywhere. "I win, I win!" she said.

"That wasn't fair," said Bonnie, but Betsy paid no
attention. She wanted to win again.

"Get dressed," Betsy said and put on her clothes
before Bonnie had even decided what to wear.

"Eat breakfast!" Betsy yelled, and she ran away.

By the time Bonnie got to the table, Betsy was already gobbling up her breakfast. "I'm done!" Betsy shouted. "I win!"

"Most of the food is on you, not in you," said Bonnie. It was true. Betsy looked very messy.

After breakfast Bonnie followed Betsy to their room.
"It's my turn to choose now," Bonnie said. She knew
that she could color in pictures better than Betsy. She
moved close to the crayons and coloring books so she
would have a head start.

"Color in the picture!" said Bonnie, grabbing one of
their many coloring books.

But Betsy grabbed all the crayons and colored in her picture very fast. She didn't even bother to stay inside the lines. "I win!" she yelled.

"You cheated!" Bonnie yelled back. "You didn't stay inside the lines."

Just then their mother came into the room. "Why don't you two go outside for a while?" she asked. "You can mail these letters for me." She gave one letter to each sister.

She opened the door wide so they could go out together. "Now play nicely," she said.

But as soon as Betsy was outside, she said, "Mail the letter!" and ran all the way to the corner without looking back. She dropped her letter into the mailbox and shouted, "I win!"

Of course, Bonnie couldn't hear her very well
because she was halfway down the block.
"Hurry up, you slowpoke!" Betsy called.

At last Bonnie got to the mailbox and mailed her letter. "You didn't wait for me," she said grumpily.

Betsy and Bonnie played in the yard all morning.
When Bonnie said she saw a dandelion, Betsy picked
it first. When Bonnie mixed mud for pies, Betsy
scooped it up and made the first pie.

"We are still playing Me First, you know," said
Betsy in a bossy voice.

At lunchtime Betsy finished all her macaroni before
Bonnie even started to eat.
"I win again!" said Betsy.

Bonnie banged her spoon down so hard that Betsy jumped. "So what if you win!" she said. "I don't care!" Her voice was angry, but her eyes were sad.

"I don't care if you win! You are mean! You are not fair! You never give me a chance! I'm not playing this game anymore." Bonnie stared at the macaroni on her plate.

Betsy was surprised. Then she began to feel bad, too. It was not fun to be first if nobody cared. It was not fun to be called bad things, especially when they were true.

"Wait a minute," said Betsy. "Do you know what?"

"What?" said Bonnie in a small voice. She was still looking down at her plate.

"You are really the winner this time," said Betsy.

"No, I'm not," said Bonnie sadly.

"Yes, you are. Because you were the first one to want to stop playing this game. I didn't want to play it anymore either, but you said so first."

Bonnie smiled as she looked at the macaroni. She said to herself very, very softly, "I win."

That night at bedtime their father came into their room. "Who wants to choose the story?" he asked.

"I do!" said Bonnie.

"I do!" said Betsy.

It made them both laugh. "She does!" they said together.

Their father smiled. "I think we can read more than one story tonight," he said.

So each sister got to choose. The stories were long, and their father's voice was gentle.

Soon Betsy began to yawn. Then Bonnie yawned, too. And, still listening, they fell asleep at the very same time.